ISBN 0-86163-394-6

© Award Publications Limited 1982
Spring House, Spring Place
Kentish Town London NW5, 3BH, England
Printed in Belgium

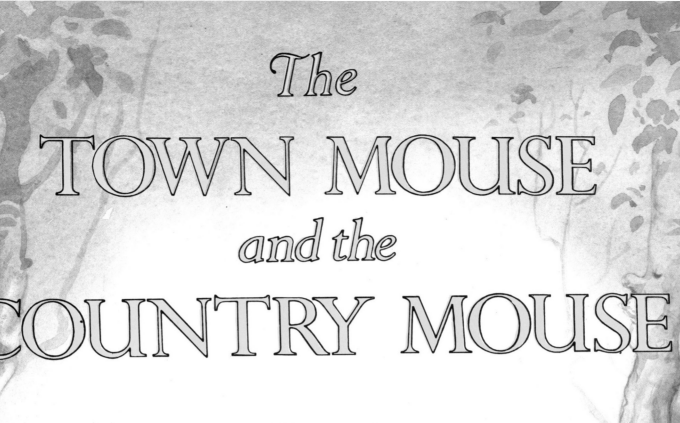

The
TOWN MOUSE
and the
COUNTRY MOUSE

Illustrated
by
Rene Cloke

AWARD PUBLICATIONS — LONDON

THE TOWN MOUSE
AND THE COUNTRY MOUSE.

The Country Mouse had invited the Town Mouse to pay him a visit. "I'm sure the country air will do you good," he told him, "and you will enjoy the beautiful scenery. The country food is most nourishing and you will find it a pleasant change after your usual rich diet.
Do come."

So the Town Mouse packed his bag and picked up his umbrella, for he never went very far without it; then he put on his top hat and started off for the country.

He found the rough lanes rather uncomfortable for walking, his feet were used to smooth pavements and he didn't like getting them muddy.

He looked in surprise at the flowers in the hedges and wondered if they were good to eat.

When he passed a village pond with a
family of ducks swimming happily about,
he stared at them in astonishment.

"Surely those are not the same birds which I find
roasted in the larder," he murmured, "and, dear me,
that must be a live rabbit!" as a young rabbit
scuttled through the hedge.

At last he reached the
Country Mouse's cottage,
a snug little nest in a
cornfield.

"Must I climb up there?"
he asked, "is it safe?"

"Of course it is," laughed the Country Mouse,
"hand me your bag and hang your umbrella on a
cornstalk — you won't want it here!"

The Town Mouse clambered up
and his friend showed him
round his nest.

"I keep my store of food in this cupboard," he said proudly, "my brush and dust-pan in that corner.

I like to keep my nest tidy and put everything in the right place.

My clothes hang on this little peg; here is my bed of hay clippings and, see, I have made up one for you by the window."

The Town Mouse thought it was all rather small and cramped but, as he was a visitor, he just nodded and said —

"Very neatly and comfortably arranged."

"Now, sit down and rest," begged the Country Mouse, "you look tired out. We will have supper at once and you will soon feel better."

The Town Mouse brightened up on hearing this and looked on eagerly as the Country Mouse spread a little check table-cloth on a toadstool table.

He took a slice of apple and two rather dry peas from the cupboard, placed two acorn cups of water side by side and, with great pride, laid an ear of corn across the table.

"Come along," he called to the Town Mouse, "you may have the apple and we will share the corn and the peas."

The Town Mouse thought that it looked a very poor meal for two people but he was too polite to say so.

He ate the piece of apple, one of the peas and nibbled at the corn.

"Is this your usual supper?" he asked.

"Well," replied the Country Mouse, "apple *and* corn at the same meal is rather special but I felt sure you would be hungry."

The Town Mouse still felt hungry when supper was over and thought longingly of the larder where he spent a good deal of his time when in the town.

"We'll take a stroll across the fields before bedtime," suggested the Country Mouse, "the fresh air will make you sleep well."

The Town Mouse considered that he had had quite enough fresh air but thought it would be bad manners to say so.

His friend pointed out many things of interest as they went along.

"See how swiftly the butterflies and dragonflies dash about," he said.

"You should see the cars and buses that go thundering down the streets in the town," replied the Town Mouse, "that would make your hair stand on end."

The Country Mouse thought that this wouldn't be very comfortable but agreed that it must be quite exciting.

Their walk took them past a field where a friendly cow gave such a loud moo over the hedge that the Town Mouse jumped with fright.

"Tell me," he squealed, "is that creature dangerous? Might it come into the cornfield and trample down your cottage?"

"No fear of that!" laughed the Country Mouse, "the farmer keeps the gate tightly closed."

In spite of the fresh air, the Town Mouse didn't sleep very well; he still felt hungry and he worried a good deal about the cow.

The Country Mouse was up at sunrise.

He tidied the nest and put a few berries and the remaining grains of corn on the table.

"Breakfast is ready," he called out, "I hope you are fond of fruit."

The Town Mouse rubbed his sleepy eyes and looked at the table.

"Fruit!" he murmured, thinking sadly of the choice pears and peaches he was used to nibbling in the larder at home. However, he did not want to hurt his friend's feelings by showing that he thought that this was a poor sort of breakfast, so he praised the flavour of the berries.

"I think I must make my way home," he said when there was nothing left on the table, "my visit has been most — er — interesting; I shall have a good deal to think about and my friends will be very eager to hear of my adventures."

The Country Mouse looked disappointed.

"I hoped you would stay a little longer," he said, "I had planned a long walk to-day and you haven't seen the view from the top of the haystack.

"You can see across the fields to the farmyard and watch the swallows feeding their young ones in the barn. There hasn't been time to show you the river where the kingfisher and the water vole live."

"You are most kind," answered the Town Mouse, hurrying down the cornstalk and collecting his umbrella, "but you must certainly come and visit me soon.

I will show you all the sights of the town and you must join my friends in a grand banquet."

This sounded most exciting and the Country Mouse said he was delighted to accept the invitation.

"Come along with me now," suggested the Town Mouse, "we shall be company for each other on the long walk."

So the Country Mouse bundled his belongings into a spotted handkerchief and the two friends started off together for the big town.

First along the country
lanes and through the wood,
then down the village street where they had to be wary of cats and
dogs.

It was getting dark by the time they reached the house where
the Town Mouse lived.

The Country Mouse was rather scared
of the traffic; it was so noisy and
dashed past them so quickly that he
felt quite bewildered.

"Is it always so busy?" he
asked "or perhaps there is
a Fair to-day," for a Fair
was the busiest thing he had
ever seen.

The Town Mouse laughed.
"Don't be nervous," he answered,
"just follow me," and he
scampered and disappeared
into a hole.

The Country Mouse followed
him along a dark passage and
found himself in the basement
kitchen of a large house.

"Quick!" whispered the
Town Mouse, "I hear the cook
coming!"

They had just time to
scuttle into a hole in the
skirting-board as the cook
rushed at them with a soup
ladle.

"Mice again!" he cried, "I
shall have to set a trap."

The two mice had to wait until midnight before the kitchen was quiet and then they crept out and made their way to the larder.

On the shelves they found a number of mice already nibbling at the food there.

There were joints of meat, fruit, jellies, cakes and cheese.

"This is my friend from the country," said the Town Mouse, "I have been paying him a visit and now I want him to see some town life. Try some of this delicious cheese, my dear fellow, it is quite harmless as long as it isn't baiting a trap!"

The Country Mouse had found the traffic
and the cook's threat of a trap so
frightening that he wished he could be
home again in the cornfield but all
the mice greeted him kindly so he
joined the feast.

The cheese was good and so was the
fruit but the other food seemed much
too rich and he really felt too nervous
to have a good appetite.

"Miau-o-o!"

"That cat again!" squealed the mice and in a momen[t] they had all vanished under the floor boards.

"This life wouldn't suit me," declared the Country Mouse to himself and he hid behind an apple as the cat looked round the door, "it may be full of thrills and excitements and there is certainly plenty to eat, but I prefer a quiet life without so many dangers.

Thank you for the delicious feast," he called out — "Good-bye, all!"

He picked up his hat and bundle, made his way out of the kitchen and started for home.

How good it was to feel the fresh air again!

The Country Mouse made his way bravely along the busy streets, hiding from prowling cats and dogs and dodging the traffic.

He reached his nest in the cornfield as the dawn was breaking and gazed out at the view.

"How beautiful it is!" he sighed as he nibbled an ear of corn, "I shall never want to roam again!"